Amelia Bedelia

Scared Silly

W9-BWB-943

Greenwillow Books, *An Imprint of HarperCollins Publishers*

Amelia Bedelia

Scared Silly

BY HERMAN PARISH PICTURES BY LYNNE AVRIL

Special thanks to Eleni Nikolopoulos for her owl expertise.

Gouache and black pencil were used to prepare the black-and-white art.
Amelia Bedelia is a registered trademark of Peppermint Partners, LLC.
Amelia Bedelia Scared Silly. Text copyright © 2021 by Herman S. Parish III. Illustrations copyright ©
2021 by Lynne Avril. All rights reserved. No part of this book may be used or reproduced in any manner
whatsoever without written permission except in the case of brief quotations embodied in critical
articles and reviews. Printed in the United States of America. For information address HarperCollins
Children's Books, a division of HarperCollins Publishers, 195 Broadway, New York, NY 10007.
www.harpercollinschildrens.com

Library of Congress Control Number: 2021938301
ISBN 978-0-06-296207-2 (hardback)—ISBN 978-0-06-296206-5 (paperback)

21 22 23 24 25 PC/BRR 10 9 8 7 6 5 4 3 2 1

 Greenwillow Books

For the real Nate the Great! —H. P.

For Jane, the Queen of Halloween!
Thanks for all your inspiration—L. A.

Amelia Bedelia

Finally

Joy

Clay

Heather

Cliff

Wade

Dawn

Skip

Angel

Penny

Candy

CONTENTS

AMELIA
BEDELIA
SCARED
SILLY

FINALLY FED UP

Amelia Bedelia draped a shiny blue cape over her shoulders and pulled a mask down over her eyes. "I was thinking that we could be superheroes for Halloween," she told Finally, her dog. "I could make you a matching cape."

Finally yawned.

"Not interested?" asked Amelia Bedelia. "I know! I think we have a pair of red shoes and a basket. How about Dorothy and Toto from *The Wizard of Oz*?"

It was Saturday afternoon, and Amelia Bedelia's bedroom was covered with craft supplies, hats, masks, scarves, and piles of dress-up clothes. There were only seven days until Halloween, and Amelia Bedelia still hadn't figured out what she and Finally were going to be. This was their very first Halloween together, and she wanted to make sure she picked an extra-special costume.

Finally jumped up onto the bed and flopped down.

"Is that a no?" Amelia Bedelia asked.

She scratched Finally's ears, then noticed something with yellow-and-black stripes peeking out from a pile. She tugged at it and held it up. It was her old sweater from when she was little. "Hmmm . . . maybe a bumblebee and a beekeeper?" She thought for a moment. "I just need to find a big hat and some netting."

Amelia Bedelia slipped the sweater over Finally's head and tugged the dog's front legs through the armholes. The sweater was a little snug, but it looked great. Amelia Bedelia rooted around on her desk and found a pair of sparkly antennas. She placed them on Finally's furry head.

Finally had had enough. She jumped

off the bed and ran downstairs.

"Finally! Stop!" Amelia Bedelia called as she raced after her. When she got to the living room, she realized that her parents, who were out in the front yard, had left the door wide open. Amelia Bedelia was just in time to catch a glimpse of Finally's tail disappearing outside.

"Oh no!" Amelia Bedelia heard her mother cry, and she got to the doorway only to see Finally run straight into the big fake spiderweb her parents were holding. Finally was going so fast that the webbing was yanked right out of their hands!

Amelia Bedelia and both her parents watched in shock as Finally raced down the front path and turned toward Maple Street. A giant fake spider was still attached to the webbing and bounced along the sidewalk. It looked like the spider was trying to catch its escaping meal.

Amelia Bedelia raced down the sidewalk after Finally. She spotted her friend Candy turning the corner up ahead. "Stop that dog!" Amelia Bedelia cried. Candy looked confused for a split second, but then quickly grabbed Finally by the sweater.

Amelia Bedelia ran to them, out of breath. "Thank you," she managed to say.

"I get to meet Finally, finally," said Candy, giving the dog a pat.

"Oh, her name's just Finally," said

Amelia Bedelia. She smiled. She was very happy to see Candy, and not just because her friend had helped catch her dog. Candy had just moved to town and was still pretty new at school. After a rocky beginning, the two girls had become fast friends. Amelia Bedelia grabbed the spiderweb and rolled it up. Then she and Candy and Finally began walking back toward Amelia Bedelia's house.

"Awesome decorations!" said Candy, taking it all in.

Amelia Bedelia smiled. She was proud that her parents were so enthusiastic about decorating their house each Halloween. She handed the web to her mother and introduced her parents to Candy.

"Pleased to meet you, Candy," said Amelia Bedelia's father as he hung vampire bats from the maple tree.

"Want to help with this spiderweb?" Amelia Bedelia's mother asked Candy.

"You don't need to ask me twice," said Candy, grabbing an end.

"She didn't," said Amelia Bedelia.

Candy turned to Amelia Bedelia. "I just love Halloween. It's my absolute favorite holiday." She sighed. "Back in Chicago there were so many fun, scary things to do. Haunted houses, midnight movie screenings, cemetery tours, an all-you-can-eat gummy-creature buffet. It was totally amazing."

"There's a lot to do here as well," said

Amelia Bedelia's mother as she attached the spiderweb to the porch railing. "Everyone decorates their houses and stores. There's a costume parade and a pumpkin-carving contest. Then when it gets dark, everyone goes trick-or-treating. It's a lot of fun."

Candy smiled politely. "That sounds nice," she said. "For the little kids. But is there anything scary for kids our age? I love to be scared on Halloween."

Amelia Bedelia racked her brain. "There is!" she said. "We totally forgot about the haunted hayride at Seven Gables Farm."

"That's right," said Amelia Bedelia's mother. "After trick-or-treating, everyone heads over to this really old farm."

"And there's a wagon full of hay bales that's pulled by horses. Everyone piles on and goes for a ride through the woods," explained Amelia Bedelia. "It's super creepy."

Her father climbed down from the ladder and joined them. "There's spooky music and ghosts and goblins and witches and monsters that jump out and scare you," he said.

"And then afterward there's a big bonfire. It's really great," finished Amelia Bedelia.

Candy nodded. "Now *that's* what I'm talking about," she said.

Amelia Bedelia laughed. "You mean that's what *we're* talking about."

"Yeah," said Candy. "I mean, it's just what the doctor ordered."

Amelia Bedelia looked at her friend. "Are you sick?"

Candy shook her head. "Nope, I feel fine. This might be my most spooktacular Halloween ever!"

HAYRIDE? NAYRIDE!

The next morning, Amelia Bedelia, her parents, and Finally were on their way to Seven Gables Farm to go pumpkin picking. The farm was run by the Hawthorne family, and had been for many generations.

"Mmmmm, I can taste apple-cider

doughnuts already!" said Amelia Bedelia's mother.

"Hey, no fair!" said Amelia Bedelia. "Did you get a doughnut earlier?"

"I didn't," said her mother. "I don't mess with family tradition. We always get doughnuts *after* we pick out our pumpkins." She smiled. "I can't wait to hear Mrs. Hawthorne's silly puns!"

"We should get more doughnuts this time," said Amelia Bedelia's father. "One measly dozen wasn't enough last year."

"You sure do have a sweet tooth," said her mother.

"What does it taste like?" asked Amelia Bedelia. "Chocolate?"

"If I did, I'd eat it," answered her father

as he made the turn into the parking lot.

"Let's go to the corn maze first!" suggested Amelia Bedelia. She loved getting lost in the tall rows of corn. It was fun figuring out how to escape.

"I think you mean the maize maze," said her father.

"Oh, Daddy," said Amelia Bedelia. "There's only one maze."

Her father laughed. "*Maize* comes from the word for corn in the language of the indigenous people of the Caribbean. It's spelled M-A-I-Z-E."

"That's amazing," said Amelia Bedelia's mother. "Utterly a-maizing!"

They arrived at the maze. Amelia Bedelia and Finally led the way in, running ahead to scope things out and then doubling back to get her parents, who moved much more slowly. But then she and Finally raced ahead a bit too far. When she turned back, she couldn't find her parents anywhere.

"They must have gone the wrong way," she said to Finally. The two of them forged ahead, but turn after turn, there were no parents to be found.

She stopped in her tracks. "Mommy?" she called out.

"Amelia Bedelia?" replied her mother. Her voice sounded close, yet far away.

"Where are you?" Amelia Bedelia hollered. "How can I get to you?"

"We somehow lost you and now we're

outside the maze," said her mother. "Are you still in there, sweetie?"

"I am!" yelled Amelia Bedelia. "How can I find my way out?"

She saw a flash of red on the ground—a lost glove. She was about to pick it up when Finally yanked her forward.

"Stay cool," called her father.

Just then a chilly breeze blew through, rustling the cornstalks and making Amelia Bedelia shiver. "That's easy. I am very cool!" she shouted.

Amelia Bedelia and Finally made a couple more turns. "I think I'm almost there," she called out. But then she glanced down. There was the same red glove. She must have gone around in a circle! "Never mind," she hollered. "I'm still really lost!"

"Hold on a minute," called her mother. "Just listen to me. You know your right from your left, right?"

Amelia Bedelia stopped. She was studying her watch and began counting down the seconds. "Fifty-nine, fifty-eight, fifty-seven." Then she asked, "Is my left right different from my regular left?"

"Nope," said her mother. "They are the same. Now I am going to teach you a trick that will get you out of any maze. Take one of your hands—right or left—and hold it against the wall of corn as you walk. Always keep that same hand on the wall. Even if you reach a dead end, just keep going with that hand on the wall. You will eventually reach the exit. Okay?"

"Okay!" Amelia Bedelia called back. "Three, two, one. Your minute is up!" She was getting worried that all the good pumpkins were going to be picked by the time she found her way out of the maze. Her stomach rumbled. She also hoped that there would be some doughnuts left. She kept her hand against the corn wall. Even when she was tempted to go another way, she remembered her mother's words. And before she knew it, she could see the exit!

"There's my girl!" said her father happily when she emerged.

"Hurry! Let's go pick the perfect pumpkin!" yelled Amelia Bedelia, taking off for the field. It felt great to be out in the open with the wide blue sky above and pumpkins as far as the eye could see. She looked around at the bright orange pumpkins nestled among the vines, in all shapes and sizes. She wasn't sure where to start.

But by the time her parents caught up to her, she had already found a pumpkin she loved, with a sturdy stem and a broad face, perfect for carving. While she helped her parents choose three more for the front of their house, she spotted the cutest little round one sitting by itself at the edge of the field. It looked lonely, so she added it to their pile. Then they

19

headed over to the farm stand.

"Hey, Mrs. Hawthorne!" Amelia Bedelia called out.

"Why, hello there, Amelia Bedelia!" Mrs. Hawthorne said, a smile spreading across her face. "Hope you guys had a *gourd* time at the farm today!" She wiped her hands on her apron and plunked their pumpkins onto a large scale. The arrow bounced back and forth for a bit until it finally came to a stop.

"Fifty-two pounds," Mrs. Hawthorne said. "A very nice haul. Will that be all?" she asked, a twinkle in her eye.

"Of course not!" said Amelia Bedelia. "We'll take two . . . no, make that *three* dozen doughnuts."

Mrs. Hawthorne laughed. "Let's hope your eyes aren't bigger than your stomach, Amelia Bedelia," she said.

"That would make a scary costume," Amelia Bedelia said.

Mrs. Hawthorne placed three bags of warm doughnuts on the counter. "I've been serving your mother my apple-cider doughnuts since she was a wee one!" Mrs. Hawthorne nodded, remembering. "I'm so glad that you are continuing the family tradition," she said. "It's fab-*boo*-lous."

Amelia Bedelia's mother paid Mrs. Hawthorne for the doughnuts and pumpkins, and some cider too. "Speaking of tradition, when will you begin the haunted hayrides this year?" she asked.

"I wish I had better news," said Mrs. Hawthorne, handing back the change. "But we had to cancel it this year."

Amelia Bedelia couldn't believe it. "Wait—no haunted hayride? Why not?"

Mrs. Hawthorne sighed. "Well, it's quite a lot of work, as I'm sure you can imagine."

Amelia Bedelia nodded. "I can."

"It got to be too much for Mr. Hawthorne and me, so fortunately, my grandson Sean took it over a couple of years ago," she continued. "But this year he's away at college, so that means no hayride."

"That's too bad," said Amelia Bedelia's father. "He did a great job."

"He really did," said Mrs. Hawthorne. "But he takes his studies seriously. Though I did tell him that all work and no play makes Jack a dull boy!"

"I thought his name was Sean," said Amelia Bedelia.

"It is," said Mrs. Hawthorne. "Sean Nathaniel Hawthorne."

"Not Jack?" asked Amelia Bedelia.

"No, it's definitely Sean," she said with a laugh.

"Well, it's too bad he has so much homework," said Amelia Bedelia. "My friend Candy was really looking forward to the haunted hayride. She loves Halloween."

"It's too bad our town doesn't have a

haunted house," said Mrs. Hawthorne. "Now that would really scare your friend silly!"

"No, that would scare her seriously!" said Amelia Bedelia. She sighed. Why couldn't their town have a real haunted house? That would make Candy happy, for sure.

COSTUMES R US

"**A**re you totally, positively sure there aren't any haunted houses in town?" Amelia Bedelia asked her mother on Monday morning before school.

"Sorry, cupcake," said her mother, handing Amelia Bedelia her lunch box and kissing her on the cheek. "But if I've told you once this weekend, I've told you a thousand times, I've lived here my whole life and I've never heard a peep from a ghost."

"That's nine hundred and ninety-seven more times than I asked," Amelia Bedelia protested. "Besides, no self-respecting ghost would peep. A real ghost sounds like this:

"*MMMMMooohWAHhannnnnn!*" wailed Amelia Bedelia.

Her mother shuddered. "That's the creepiest cry I ever heard," she said.

"Let me know if you hear that sound," said Amelia Bedelia, slinging her backpack over her shoulder and heading out the front door.

"If I hear a howl like that, you can find me under my bed," said Amelia Bedelia's mother.

Reaching the sidewalk, Amelia Bedelia turned around to wave goodbye to her mom standing in the doorway. Amelia Bedelia smiled at the sight of her own haunted house. Spooky spiderwebs stretched from the bushes up the steps to the front door, where a giant spider perched overhead. Vampire bats hung from the maple branches, ready to swoop down. The pumpkins that she and her parents had carved grinned at her ghoulishly.

Amelia Bedelia had one more pumpkin

to carve, but she wouldn't carve that one until the competition on Halloween. Each year there were prizes awarded for the silliest, the funniest, the scariest, and the most original pumpkins. Amelia Bedelia had never won. She hoped this would be her year.

A gust of wind set the bats' wings flapping. Amelia Bedelia shivered, zipped up her hoodie, and headed to school. Maybe she'd carve a bat into her pumpkin. That would be very scary indeed.

Mrs. Shauk stood in front of the class, writing on the whiteboard. "If Heather has thirteen pumpkins, and Pat gives her eighteen more, but then I accidentally knock over six of them, what do we have?"

Joy raised her hand, but Cliff blurted out his answer first. "Pumpkin soup!"

Everyone laughed.

"Good one," said Clay. "Hey, how do you fix a broken jack-o'-lantern?"

Mrs. Shauk sighed. "I give up, Clay. How *do* you fix a broken jack-o'-lantern?"

"With a pumpkin patch!" Clay said.

The class laughed, even louder this time.

Mrs. Shauk put her finger to her lips. "I know you're excited because it's almost Halloween, but you need to settle down. You're loud enough to wake the dead!"

Amelia Bedelia shook her head. "That's impossible, Mrs. Shauk. Plus, the cemetery is way on the other side of town."

Mrs. Shauk threw up her hands. "See! You're all obsessed with Halloween!" She glanced at the clock on the classroom wall. "I give up," she said.

"Again?" said Amelia Bedelia.

Mrs. Shauk sighed. "Tell me about your costumes."

"All right!" said Clay. "I'll give you a clue." He jumped out of his seat, stretched out his arms, and began to shuffle around the classroom, groaning.

"A mummy?" guessed Holly.

"Someone with a bad stomachache who ate too much candy corn?" guessed Skip.

"Don't go as a zombie," said Candy.

"Because that's what I'm going to be."

Clay stopped in his tracks, looking disgruntled. "I'm Frankenstein!" he said huffily.

Mrs. Shauk corrected him. "I think you mean Frankenstein's monster. Frankenstein is the name of the doctor who built the creature. It's from a book written by Mary Shelley in 1818."

"Shauk the Hawk knows everything," Amelia Bedelia whispered to Candy.

"Not everything, Amelia Bedelia," said Mrs. Shauk, without turning around. "But almost!"

Amelia Bedelia jumped. Everyone said that Mrs. Shauk had eyes in the back of her head.

"Mary Shelley! You mean a girl made up that gruesome story?" said Wade.

"Girls can do anything," said Penny. "I'm going to be a doctor for Halloween. I have a lab coat and a real stethoscope."

"Big surprise," said Cliff, rolling his eyes.

"That's not a surprise at all," said Amelia Bedelia. "Penny wants to be a doctor when she grows up."

Angel raised her hand.

"Yes, Angel?" said Mrs. Shauk.

"My dad made me a suit of armor out of cardboard and tin foil," she said. "I'm going to be a knight!"

Pat was going to be a chef. Rose told everyone about her unicorn costume.

Holly had decided to be Sherlock Holmes, and Heather was going to be Watson. Cliff was going to be a cowboy. Dawn, who had just gotten a new pair of skates, was planning to be a roller-skating witch. Teddy was going to be a clown.

"Ooh, spooky!" said Candy with a shiver.

Teddy looked confused. "No, funny," he said. "Clowns are funny."

"Not in my book," said Candy.

"Did you write a book like Mary Shelley about a scary clown?" asked Wade.

Amelia Bedelia stared at Candy. She had no idea her new friend had written a book!

"I'm going to combine a cow costume

with an angel costume," said Joy, "so I can make heavenly ice cream."

"I'm going to be a daisy," said Daisy.

Amelia Bedelia had no idea what Joy was talking about, but she loved Daisy's daisy idea.

"Hey, Candy, maybe you should be a candy bar, " suggested Skip.

"No way," said Candy. "I like scary costumes. The spookier the better."

"How about you, Amelia Bedelia?" asked Mrs. Shauk.

"I don't know yet," Amelia Bedelia replied. "I'm still figuring out the perfect costume for Finally and me."

"Like my grandpa says, it's time to fish or cut bait," said Chip.

"Sounds smelly to me! I don't have time for that," said Amelia Bedelia. "I've got to come up with a costume, and fast."

"My grandpa means that it's time to make up your mind," said Chip.

"I know!" said Amelia Bedelia.

Mrs. Shauk turned to Candy. "Are you looking forward to your first Halloween with us, Candy?" she asked.

Candy nodded. "I sure am," she said. "I can't wait for the haunted hayride!"

The whole class cheered. Everyone loved the haunted hayride.

Amelia Bedelia put her head on her desk and groaned. Her friends turned to stare at her.

"What's wrong, Amelia Bedelia?"

asked Mrs. Shauk. "You look like you lost your best friend."

Amelia Bedelia shook her head. "No, my friends are all right here. I'm just sad because I have some bad news." She looked down at her shoes.

"Spit it out," said Cliff.

Amelia Bedelia made a face. "Eww," she said. "That is so gross. I'll just say it. There isn't going to be a haunted hayride this year."

SCARING UP A GHOST

Candy yelled, "Noooooooooooo!"

Holly fell off her chair and bumped right into Amelia Bedelia. "Sorry," she said. "I nearly jumped out of my skin."

"I'm glad you didn't," said Amelia Bedelia. She looked over at Candy.

"This is horrible!" Candy wailed. "I was

really looking forward to a super-spooky Halloween, like we had in Chicago."

The bell rang for recess. Everyone grabbed jackets and sweaters and began to file out the door.

"Candy, would you stay behind for a minute, please?" asked Mrs. Shauk.

Candy, still looking upset, sat back down in her seat.

Amelia Bedelia walked past the swings and slide and the foursquare court and went straight to the tree stump they used as a meeting table. Her friends followed behind her.

"I hope Candy isn't in trouble," said Daisy.

"She really lost her temper," said Heather.

"It looked more like she found it," said Amelia Bedelia.

Dawn looked around the playground. "Hey, has anyone seen Holly?" she asked.

Just then the door burst open and Holly came running out. She raced to the tree stump table, out of breath. "I was in the coat closet, trying to find my jacket, and I overheard Candy and Mrs. Shauk talking," she said. She bit her lip.

"Is Candy in trouble?" asked Dawn.

"No, it's worse than that," said Holly. "I heard Candy tell Mrs. Shauk that maybe she would go back to Chicago."

"Oh no!" said Amelia Bedelia. "That's terrible news."

"We have to convince her to stay," said Rose.

"But how?" asked Penny.

"I know," said Cliff. "We need to do something really scary."

"Cool," said Clay. "Like what?"

Amelia Bedelia shook her head. "I asked my mom this weekend if there are any haunted houses or ghosts in our town. But she said there aren't."

"Ghost stories are pretend anyway," said Joy with a shrug. "Let's just make one up for her."

"What a great idea, Joy!" said Amelia Bedelia.

Clay stuck his arms straight out in front of him. "As Frankenstein . . ."

"Frankenstein's monster!" shouted Amelia Bedelia and her friends.

"As Frankenstein's monster, I think I'm the perfect person to tell it," Clay continued.

"Well, get ready, because here comes Candy," warned Heather.

Candy had spotted everyone and was heading over. "Sorry for yelling," she said. "I was just super disappointed to hear about the hayride. Guess we're in for a boring Halloween this year, huh?"

"Maybe not," said Amelia Bedelia, poking Clay in the back. "Clay, don't you have something to tell Candy?"

Clay jumped. "Yup," he said. "Our town is haunted!"

Candy perked right up. "Really?" she asked. "Why didn't you tell me before?"

Clay cleared his throat, suddenly not looking quite so sure of himself. "So . . . um . . . once upon a time in our town there was this guy. And . . . something very scary happened to him and then . . . um . . . there was a ghost. . . ." His voice trailed off.

Daisy leaned over and whispered in Amelia Bedelia's ear. "Clay's got stage fright!" she said.

Amelia Bedelia glanced at Clay. "He's not on a stage," she whispered back to Daisy. "I think he's just nervous."

Everyone waited patiently for Clay to

continue his story. But he just stood there in silence. Amelia Bedelia looked over at Candy, who was stifling a yawn. Oh no! Amelia Bedelia jumped up. She had no idea what she was going to say, but it *had* to be better than Clay's story.

"Thanks for starting the story, Clay," she said. He looked at her gratefully and sat down. But what was she going to say? She took a deep breath and began to talk, making it up as she went along. "Years and years ago, our town used to have an inn for weary travelers."

"What was it called?" asked Candy. Her eyes were gleaming.

Amelia Bedelia looked around wildly. "It was called the . . . the Swing Inn."

"The Swing Inn?" said Candy.

Amelia Bedelia nodded. "The Swing Inn. There were no cars back then, so everyone traveled on horseback. It took a long time to go even short distances, and it was dangerous to travel in the woods at night. So when the sun went down, people would stop and spend the night at an inn. They would eat dinner, feed their horses, and get a good night's sleep. Most inns were run by people who were kind and generous. But the Swing Inn was owned by a mean old man. He kicked puppies, stole from the collection basket at church, and made mean faces at babies to make them cry. Nobody in town liked him at all."

"What was his name?" asked Candy eagerly.

Boy, Candy was really into the details! Amelia Bedelia paused. "His name was—"

"Ebenezer Scrooge?" offered Wade.

"Um, yeah, that's right, Ebenezer Scrooge," said Amelia Bedelia. The name sounded familiar, but she wasn't sure where she had heard it before.

"Ebenezer Scrooge?" Candy asked. "Are you sure? Scrooge sounds more like Christmas than Halloween."

Amelia Bedelia nodded. "Did I say Scrooge? I meant to say Sludge! Anyway, he was mean and grouchy. Well, one chilly night, under a full moon, a weary traveler rode into town looking for a place to rest.

He saw the sign for the Swing Inn and felt very happy. He was tired and hungry, and his horse needed some oats and some water. He knocked on the door . . ."

She paused to knock on the tree stump table. *Knock-knock-knock.*

". . . and it swung open with a loud *creeeeeaaaaaakkkkkk*."

"Ooh, I'm getting goose bumps," squealed Rose.

Amelia Bedelia turned to look at Rose, but Rose was wearing a jacket and long pants. She went right back to the story.

"'What do you want?' Ebenezer growled.

"'A bed for the night, and a barn for my horse,' said the traveler.

"'Show me your money,' said Ebenezer.

"'I don't have any,' said the traveler.

"'Well then, you can't stay here," said Ebenezer. And he started to shut the door.

"'But I'm so hungry,' said the traveler, stopping the door with his foot. 'If I could just have one of those—'"

Crunch! Amelia Bedelia looked at Pat, who had just bitten into a shiny red apple.

"'—apples,'" Amelia Bedelia continued. "Ebenezer had an apple orchard and always kept a big basket of apples by his front door. He liked to throw the rotten ones at the neighborhood kids. But even though he had apples right there, Ebenezer laughed, grabbed the basket of apples, and slammed the door in the traveler's face.

"'Please let me in,' the man begged, pounding on the door. 'I'm so tired. My horse needs a rest. It's dark and scary in the woods. I'm afraid. Please let me in.'

"'Too bad!' yelled Ebenezer through the door. 'Begone with you! There's another inn at the next town. Maybe they give out charity, but I do not!' And he locked the door and went to bed. The traveler knocked and knocked, begging for mercy, until he finally gave up. He got back on his horse and headed off into the dark night."

Amelia Bedelia glanced around the stump table. Her friends stared back at her, eyes wide.

"What happened next?" asked Candy. "You're on a roll."

Amelia Bedelia checked her soles for bread crumbs, then continued.

"The next day the horse returned, but the saddle was empty. Everyone blamed Ebenezer, but he didn't care. Not one bit. That night there was a knock on the door."

Amelia Bedelia knocked on the tree stump. *Knock-knock-knock*.

"'Go away!' Ebenezer called. The knocking got louder. *Knock-knock-knock*. But when Ebenezer opened the door, there was no one there.

"It happened night after night. And each time, when Ebenezer stepped outside to see who was knocking, he would hear hoofbeats getting closer and closer . . . but the road was always empty. Ebenezer started telling people that the ghost of the missing traveler was after him. He promised that he'd let the man in this time, and feed him, and let him stay for free. He was desperate to get rid of the curse.

"Soon after that, he took down the inn's sign and locked himself inside. But the hoofbeats and the knocking continued. People could see Ebenezer's candle shaking as he peered fearfully out the window. Then one night someone heard a terrible racket coming from the Swing Inn. Knocking and yelling and the pounding of horse hooves.

"The next morning the innkeeper was found in his doorway. He was dead of fright. His hair had turned snow white."

Amelia Bedelia lowered her voice. "And in his hand, he held . . . a single apple."

Candy's eyes were shining. "Spooky!" she said. "I had no idea this town was haunted! Is the inn still standing? Where is it?"

"I . . . um . . ." Amelia Bedelia had no idea what to say. Thankfully, the bell rang. She breathed a sigh of relief. She had never been so happy for recess to be over in her life. But it was nice to see Candy smiling again. Maybe her spooky ghost story had convinced her new friend to stay!

WHOOOOO'S THERE?

"**O**kay, class," said Ms. Garcia that afternoon in science class. "We are starting a
new unit today. We are going to study a
very fascinating creature that is quite
popular this time of year. It has large
eyes and long, sharp—"

"I know!" shouted Clay. "Mrs. Shauk!"

Ms. Garcia tried not to laugh. "No, it is mostly seen at night."

"I know!" shouted Cliff. "A vampire!"

"Mrs. Shauk is right," said Ms. Garcia. "You guys *do* have Halloween on the brain! Let me give you some more clues. It flies silently through the air and preys on unsuspecting—"

"Students!" said Clay. "Still sounds like Mrs. Shauk."

"Or a vampire," said Teddy.

"Well, how about this?" said Ms. Garcia. "There are two hundred different species of this bird of prey in the world. It can't move its eyes, but its head can turn two hundred seventy degrees or more."

"Almost completely around!" said Penny.

Amelia Bedelia and her friends tried turning their heads around, looking at one another and shrugging their shoulders. None of them had any clue until Mrs. Garcia gave them one last hint.

"Whooooooo could it be?"

"An owl !" said Angel right away.

"That's right," said Ms. Garcia. "Owls are found on every continent except Antarctica. They come in all sizes, ranging from the six-inch-tall elf owl to the thirty-two-inch-tall great gray owl. And the females are larger and more aggressive than the males."

"Just like falcons," Skip said.

"And all birds of prey," added Ms. Garcia. "Now, can anyone tell us why an owl's feathers are such dull colors?"

"I know!" shouted Chip. "For sabotage."

Amelia Bedelia frowned. That didn't sound quite right.

Mrs. Garcia smiled. "Very close, Chip. I think you mean *camouflage*. Owls are excellent hunters. Their muted feathers help them blend in with their surroundings. They have keen eyesight. A northern hawk owl can spot a mouse up to half a mile away."

"But they can't see very well up close," added Joy.

Ms. Garcia nodded. "So they rely on

their incredible hearing." She dimmed the classroom lights. "Now I'd like you all to close your eyes and pretend you are walking through the woods at dusk. I'm going to play the sounds of different owls' calls. I think you'll be surprised by the variety of sounds they make."

The class was perfectly silent. They listened intently as the recording began and various owls began to hoot. But that wasn't all they heard. The owls also chirped, whistled, hissed, whinnied, barked, and growled.

"There's one more," said Ms. Garcia. "Get ready for it." An ear-piercing shriek echoed through the classroom, and everyone jumped. Ms. Garcia smiled again. "Nothing like the call of a barn owl," she said. "It can sound just like a person screaming."

She switched the lights back on. "Now, make sure not to wear your best clothes tomorrow. We're going to do a special activity, and it might get a little messy."

"Give us a hint!" begged Rose.

But Ms. Garcia just shook her head. "I don't want to ruin the surprise," she said. "I'm so glad you all give a hoot about owls!" she said.

"Hoot! Hoot!" said Amelia Bedelia.

Amelia Bedelia's father stared at her from across the table. "I'm trying to keep a straight face," he said. "But you're making it pretty hard."

"Your face doesn't look crooked to me, Daddy," said Amelia Bedelia. She picked up her fork to dig into the lasagna her father had made. But the fork clattered onto her plate, slipping through her gauze-covered fingers. She had been right in the middle of wrapping herself and Finally up as mummies when her mother called her down to dinner.

Her mother reached over and unrolled the gauze around Amelia Bedelia's right hand. "You might want to uncover your mouth as well," she suggested.

"Maybe this costume isn't such a good idea," said Amelia Bedelia. "I won't be able to eat any candy on Halloween."

"Or see very well," added her father. "So, did you break the news to Candy about the haunted hayride?"

"I didn't break anything," said Amelia Bedelia. "But I told her."

"What did she say?" asked her father.

"You really want to know?" asked Amelia Bedelia.

Her parents nodded.

So she stood up, took a deep breath, and began howling at the top of her lungs.

"Arrooooooooooooo!" Finally joined in.

Her parents covered their ears.

"Not happy, huh," said Amelia Bedelia's father.

"Candy even told Mrs. Shauk that she was thinking about moving back to Chicago," said Amelia Bedelia. "But then I told her a spooky story at recess, and that seemed to make her happy."

Her father shivered.

"Are you chilly?" asked Amelia Bedelia.

"Hasn't that ever happened to you?" he asked. "When you shiver for no reason?"

"I guess so," said Amelia Bedelia. "But why does it happen?"

"La morte è passata," he replied.

"Huh?" said Amelia Bedelia. "Pass more pasta?"

"La morte è passata," repeated her father. "It's an old Italian saying. It means that Death has just passed by you. That's what makes you shiver."

Amelia Bedelia and her mother looked at each other. They both shuddered at the same time.

"That is so creepy," said Amelia Bedelia.

Her father shrugged, like it was no big deal. He leaned down to untangle Finally's paw caught in gauze.

"Looks like it's back to the drawing board on the costume, sweetie," said her mother.

Amelia Bedelia shook her head. "I don't want to be an artist."

As soon as Amelia Bedelia was done with dinner, she began unwrapping herself. There were a lot of layers of gauze to untangle. "This is going to take forever," she said.

"Need your mummy?" asked her father.

"To unravel you?" her mother finished.

Amelia Bedelia looked at her parents. Then they all burst out laughing.

"Hey, Amelia Bedelia, want to play foursquare?" Daisy asked the next day at recess.

"Sure!" said Amelia Bedelia. But just as they were about to start the game, someone grabbed her arm. She turned around. It was Candy.

"Please tell us another ghost story?" Candy asked. "You're so good at it."

"Um, okay," said Amelia Bedelia.

Amelia Bedelia hoped she would be inspired on the walk across the playground. By the time they reached the stump, a group of her friends had gathered, eager for more spooky tales as well. But Amelia Bedelia's mind was a complete blank.

Candy plopped down next to the stump and rested her elbows on it. "So where is this inn, exactly?" she asked. "Can we visit it after we go trick-or-treating? We can hunt for ghosts." She hugged herself. "That would be the spookiest Halloween ever!"

"I—I . . . um . . . ," stammered Amelia Bedelia. She hadn't planned for this.

Maybe telling Candy ghost stories wasn't such a great idea after all!

"Ready when you are," said Candy.

"Um . . . uh,"stalled Amelia Bedelia.

Then Holly spoke up. "I know this story, Amelia Bedelia. Let me tell it.

"After Ebenezer died, the truth came out. The traveler hadn't disappeared. Some neighbors of Ebenezer's had taken pity on the traveler and had given him and his horse a place to spend the night. The neighbors, tired of Ebenezer being mean all the time, had decided to teach him a lesson. But they went too far and scared him to death. Ebenezer had no heirs, so the inn went up for auction, and one of the neighbors bought it for a song."

"Wow," said Amelia Bedelia. "I didn't know you could do that. He must have been a good singer."

"The neighbor—his name was Mr. Gory—painted the inn and put up a new sign, and he was just about to open it for business. But that very night, as a full moon rose in the sky, Mr. Gory awoke with a start. There was a terrible racket. Someone was banging on the inn door. But when he opened it, no one was there.

"He got back into bed, pulled up the covers, and went back to sleep. But a few minutes later he awoke with a start. Someone was shaking him violently. And before his unbelieving eyes stood

the ghost of Ebenezer, in his long nightshirt, holding a candle. 'Help me!' Ebenezer begged. 'Make him go away!'

"Mr. Gory was terrified. He ran out of the house, screaming his head off. But when he and the rest of the neighbors returned at dawn, the inn had been burned to the ground. In the smoking ashes, they found just one thing—a gleaming red apple."

Amelia Bedelia looked at Candy. Now her new friend had a big smile on her face.

"Cool! A baked apple," Candy said.

Heather leaned over. "Holly really saved our bacon," she said softly in Amelia Bedelia's ear.

Amelia Bedelia gave Heather a funny look. "Never mind breakfast," she whispered back. "She totally took care of our haunted house problem!"

SEE YOU LATER, REGURGITATOR!

"**W**e are going to have a special guest this afternoon," said Ms. Garcia the next day in science. "Someone who really appreciates birds of prey and wants to participate in our class activity." Amelia Bedelia and her friends looked at one another. Who could it be?

There was a knock at the door. Angel, who was closest, got up to open it. The class gasped as Mrs. Shauk walked in.

"They don't call me Shauk the Hawk for nothing," said Mrs. Shauk, squeezing herself into an empty desk chair.

"What is the mystery activity?" Joy asked, once their teacher was settled in.

Ms. Garcia smiled. "It's a very special one. It's really perfect for you Halloween fans. It has to do with owl nutrition. What do you think owls like to eat?" she asked.

"Mice?" said Pat.

"And other rodents," added Joy.

"How about bugs?" suggested Penny.

"Anything else?" asked Ms. Garcia.

The class was silent.

Mrs. Shauk raised her hand.

"Yes, Mrs. Shauk?" said Ms. Garcia.

"Depending on their size," she said, "owls eat all those things, and snakes, fish, birds, frogs—even other small mammals."

"Very good," said Ms. Garcia. "As we know, owls have beaks," she continued. "But what *don't* they have?"

"Whiskers?" guessed Wade.

"That's true," said Ms. Garcia. "But I was thinking more of something they would eat with."

"Silverware," said Cliff.

Everyone laughed.

"Oh, I know," said Joy. "Teeth!"

"That's right. Owls do not have teeth. That means that they can't chew their food. So they tear it with their beaks and sometimes even swallow it whole. Then they digest the digestible parts. But the parts that they can't digest, like bones and teeth and fur and feathers, are formed into pellets, which is what we are going to dissect today."

"Wait a minute," said Skip. "Are you saying that we're going to cut up owl poop?"

Ms. Garcia held up a hand. "After the nutrients have been absorbed, the owl then regurgitates the pellets. So it's actually more like owl vomit."

"I'm going to lose my lunch!" said Dawn.

"Don't worry," said Amelia Bedelia.

"If that ever happened, I'd share mine with you."

"Now, the pellets come to us sterilized, but to be extra cautious we are going to wear protective gloves. Mrs. Shauk will be handing out newspaper. After you cover your desk, you will get a pellet, some toothpicks, tweezers, and a magnifying glass. You should take your pellet apart carefully with the toothpicks. Then pick out the contents with the tweezers and discover what your owl had for dinner! The bones are very delicate, so be careful. You may also find feathers, fur, and other objects. You'll each get a chart so you can identify which bones belong to which animal. These are barn owl pellets, so be prepared to find lots of rodents."

"Could we find a pearl?" said Teddy.

"No, owls don't eat oysters," said Heather.

"This is so cool!" said Clay, giving Heather a high five.

Penny got straight to work, taking apart her pellet with precision.

The other students were slower to get started. Rose looked especially disgusted. But before long, everyone was intently dissecting their pellets.

"Look at those tiny ribs!" Penny exclaimed.

Amelia Bedelia took a deep breath and studied her pellet. It was oval, dark, and dry looking, only a couple of inches

long. Luckily, it didn't smell at all. She began to pull it apart with her toothpicks. The insides were dense, almost like the lint in the dryer at home. After gently rooting around, she spotted something. She picked it up with her tweezers and examined it through the magnifying glass. It was a skull, tiny and delicate. She held up the chart and tried to make a match. She was pretty sure it belonged to a vole, whatever that was.

By the end of the class, everyone was quite pleased with themselves. Mrs. Shauk had assembled an almost complete mouse skeleton. "No bones about it," she said, "that was a great activity. Thanks for letting me bone up on owls with you today."

"Oh, there's more to come!" said Ms. Garcia. She was standing by the door, handing out sheets of paper. "Get these permission slips signed by your parents. We're going on an owl walk at Culloden Point Park on Friday evening." She turned to Mrs. Shauk. "You're invited to come too, of course."

Mrs. Shauk smiled. "We're going to have a great time," she said. "I can feel it in my bones!"

Amelia Bedelia winced. That sounded super painful to her. Ouch!

"Did you know that owls throw up pellets full of the parts of their food they can't digest?" Amelia Bedelia said that evening at dinner. "Like bones and skulls and beaks?"

"Oh my," said her mother, setting down her fork.

"As a general rule, we avoid talking about vomit at the dinner table," said her father. He got a twinkle in his eye. "Maybe you could say that the owl upchucked? Or tossed its cookies?"

Amelia Bedelia shook her head. "Owls don't eat cookies, Daddy," she said. "They eat rodents and bugs, plus snakes, fish, birds, frogs, and even small mammals. Everyone dissected their very own owl pellet today in science class. Even Mrs. Shauk. Mine had a vole skull in it, and some bones. Oh, and a little bit of fur too. It was pretty awesome."

"Hey, puddin'," said her mother.

"Have you figured out your costume yet? It's almost Halloween!"

"Not yet," said Amelia Bedelia. "But I found a pink dress from when I was little, so I was thinking Finally could be a princess and I could wear my green pajamas and a crown and be a prince that turned into a fr—" She narrowed her eyes at her mother. "Hey, are you trying to change the subject?" she asked.

"You bet your boots," her mother replied.

Amelia Bedelia looked down at her feet. "Now why would I want to do that?" she asked.

CANDY LOVES CANDIES

"I'm ready for another ghost story," said Candy the next day at recess. Amelia Bedelia and her friends stared at one another. Amelia Bedelia bit her lip. And then, finally, to everyone's relief, Joy spoke up.

"It was many, many years after the

Swing Inn burned down," she started. "A mother and her daughter were on a road trip, driving through town. It started to rain, lightly at first, and then harder and harder. Soon they couldn't see out the car windows. They pulled over, and to their great relief, saw a sign for an inn through the mist.

"They parked and ran inside. The innkeeper said he had a nice room for them. They were tired, so they went straight to bed. The next morning, they couldn't find the innkeeper anywhere, so they wrote a note thanking him, put the money they owed on a table, and left.

"They were hungry, so they went to

84

a local diner for breakfast. The waitress was friendly, and they began chatting. When she found out that they were on a road trip she said, 'I hope you weren't driving through that terrible rain last night.'

"'Oh no,' the mother replied. 'We found the inn here and stayed the night.'

"The waitress shook her head. 'Our town doesn't have an inn. You must have stayed in another town.'

"'No,' said the daughter. 'We stayed here, at the Swing Inn.'

"The waitress laughed. 'Oh, you're joking!' she said. 'The Swing Inn burned down almost a hundred years ago.' The mother and daughter tried to argue, but the waitress insisted that the Swing Inn was no more.

"They quickly finished their breakfast and decided to go find the inn and prove the waitress wrong. They drove back and forth several times but couldn't find it. Finally they got out of the car and walked to the place they were sure the inn had been.

"All they found was rubble and an old foundation that smelled of smoke. But there, on the ground, sat their money and their note. And right next to it . . . a shiny red apple."

"Oooooh, that made me shiver!" said Candy, rubbing her arms.

"Pass more pasta," said Amelia Bedelia.

"What?" asked Candy. "Where's the pasta?"

"Never mind," said Amelia Bedelia. It was too complicated to explain.

"Hey," said Teddy. "I heard that my dentist, Dr. Dixon, is handing out toothbrushes to trick-or-treaters."

"Another house to add to our Do Not Visit list," said Penny.

"Who else is on the Do Not Visit list?" asked Candy.

"Well, Mrs. Martin gives out pennies, and the Bridgers always hand out boxes of raisins," Teddy explained.

Candy made a face. "Yikes," she said.

"But we know all the houses to hit first,"

Dawn assured her. "Like the Bhagats. They give full-size candy bars every year. You want to get there before they run out. Stick with us. We have a system that never fails."

"I love candy," said Candy.

Amelia Bedelia and her friends laughed.

"Who doesn't?" asked Amelia Bedelia.

The bell rang. Recess was over.

Skip was the first to arrive back at the classroom. He gasped. "What—?" He stopped short, and Amelia Bedelia bumped right into him. She peered around him. There was a single apple sitting in front of the classroom door.

"But—but . . . ," stammered Pat.

"It's the ghost of Ebenezer!" whispered Rose.

Amelia Bedelia nudged her. "Did you forget we made the whole thing up?" she whispered.

Heather approached Skip. "Did you put that there, trying to scare us?" she asked.

"Yeah, Skip, are you up to your old tricks?" asked Holly.

"He's not a magician," said Amelia Bedelia.

"I never said he was a magician," said Holly. "But he used to be a practical joker!"

"Then he'd be up to his old jokes, not tricks," argued Amelia Bedelia.

Skip took a step back. "I'm not up to any jokes *or* tricks," he said. "I'm as scared as you are!"

"I'm not scared, and I'm not falling for

this," said Joy. "I wasn't born yesterday."

"You were born the same year as me," said Amelia Bedelia. Then she felt another pass-more-pasta shiver. She hugged herself tight. Could their town really be haunted?

BUT THE TRICKER IS QUICKER

"You have a great time, sweetie," said Amelia Bedelia's father as she unbuckled her seat belt and flung open the car door.

"Hey, Amelia Bedelia!" called Chip.

Amelia Bedelia waved and headed over to join her friends. They were waiting for the bus that would take them to the park for their owl walk. It felt strange to be waiting for a school bus in the dark. At last it pulled up, coming to a stop with a squeal of its brakes.

"Hello, Ms. Chang," Amelia Bedelia sang out to the bus driver as she bounded up the steps to be the first on board.

"Hello, Amelia Bedelia," Ms. Chang replied. "You must have ants in your pants tonight!"

Amelia Bedelia laughed. "No I don't!" she said. How uncomfortable would *that* be? She walked to the back of the bus where the bounciest seats were. She sat down and scooted toward the window.

"Is this seat taken?" asked Dawn.

Amelia Bedelia looked at her friend.

"No," she said, patting the seat next to her. "It's still here."

Dawn plopped down just as the bus lurched forward. "That was so weird yesterday," she said. "Do you think our ghost stories are coming true?"

Amelia Bedelia shook her head. "When I got home from school, I told my parents what happened. They think it's just someone playing a trick."

"That's what my dad said too," said Dawn. She shrugged. "They're probably right."

"It's too weird otherwise," said Amelia Bedelia.

"And scary," added Dawn.

"But who is it?" asked Amelia Bedelia.

Dawn shook her head. "I have no idea."

"Psst! Psst!" said Cliff, turning around in his seat. "Who wants to hear a ghost story?"

"I don't think I do," said Penny. "After what happened yesterday."

"Oh, I think you'll all like this one," Cliff said. "It's a story from right before the Swing Inn burned down." He motioned to Clay.

"So the neighbor who bought the inn, Mr. Gory, had spent all day painting and renovating, and he was very tired. He got into bed and was reading a book by candlelight, when suddenly he heard a sound downstairs. He sat bolt upright. 'Who's there?' he called."

"'I am the ghost of the bloody finger, in the living room,'" Clay rasped in a scratchy whisper.

Dawn scooted closer to Amelia Bedelia.

"Mr. Gory gasped and pulled the blankets to his chin," said Cliff. "But the voice was coming closer."

"'I am the ghost of the bloody finger, on the stairs,'" Clay growled.

"'Go away!' Mr. Gory begged. 'Just go away!' But the voice was getting even closer," said Cliff, waggling his eyebrows.

Clay continued. "'I am the ghost of the bloody finger, in the hallway!'"

"Mr. Gory pulled the covers over his head," said Cliff. "He could hardly breathe. And the voice was closer still."

Clay's voice rose. "'I am the ghost of the bloody finger, in the bedroom.'"

"'Leave me alone, please,' Mr. Gory begged," whispered Cliff. "And the voice said . . .'"

"'Do you have a Band-Aid?'" finished Clay.

The bus was quiet. Everyone stared at Cliff and Clay for a moment. Then they all burst out laughing.

Except for Candy. "I only like *scary* ghost stories," she said.

When they arrived at Culloden Point Park, a ranger was waiting for them in the parking lot. Amelia Bedelia could just make out her crisp brown-and-green uniform in the dim light. A brimmed hat sat on her long, dark hair, which was pulled back in a ponytail. There was a flashlight on her belt and a backpack slung over her shoulder.

"Hello, everyone," she said. "My name is Ranger Eleni, and I will be taking you on your owl walk tonight."

"Hello, Ranger Eleni," said Ms. Garcia. "We're so excited to be here. We've been studying owls all week, and we're really hoping to see one tonight."

"Me too," said Ranger Eleni. "Here's the plan. We are going to walk a short distance into the woods. I'll light the way with my flashlight, and we need to stay close together. Once we arrive, I'll shut off my flashlight and get my spotlight ready. It will be quite dark, and we'll have to be very quiet. This time of year, we're most likely to see young screech owls, so I'll be playing a recording of a screech owl call. Hopefully, one will hear it and fly over to investigate.

"Listen carefully, because as I'm sure you know, owls are very quiet flyers. If an owl lands nearby, I'll shine my spotlight on it. It will freeze when the light hits its eyes, so hopefully you'll all be able to get a good look. But we won't keep it in the spotlight too long, so stay alert!" She clapped her hands together. "Are you ready to go?"

"Whoooooo-ray!" said Penny.

Amelia Bedelia and her friends nodded silently. They were already practicing being quiet.

Everyone followed Ranger Eleni out of the parking lot and onto a trail that led into the woods. Someone stepped on a dry twig.

SSSNAPPPPP!

Suddenly there was an explosive sound of beating wings. A shadowy flock of birds took off into the air. *Caw-caw-caw!*

They all jumped, even Ranger Eleni.

"That bunch of crows really scared me!" exclaimed Dawn.

"A murder of crows," said Ranger Eleni.

Amelia Bedelia looked at her friends, eyes wide.

"We weren't trying to murder them," said Clay quickly. "We never touched a feather."

Ranger Eleni chuckled. "No, a group of crows is called a murder," she explained. "Groups of birds have strange and interesting names. Have you heard of a gaggle of geese?"

Almost everyone had.

"And do you know what a group of owls is called?"

"I know!" said Cliff. "A pellet party!"

The friends laughed.

"Actually," said Ranger Eleni, "a group of owls is called a parliament."

"Like the government of England?" asked Joy.

"That's right," said Ranger Eleni. "Guess what a group of eagles is called?" After no one answered, she gave them a hint. "An eagle is the symbol of the United States. Here's a clue: Who makes our laws?"

"Congress!" said Chip. "Is it a congress of eagles?"

"You got it," said Ranger Eleni.

"Every group should have a cool name," said Holly. "Like a group of teachers should be called a . . . task."

Mrs. Shauk nodded. "A task of teachers. That works for me. And how about a stable of students?"

"And a raft of rangers!" added Penny.

"I like that!" Ranger Eleni laughed. She led them into a clearing. "Here we are," she said. "Now as soon as everyone is ready, I'll turn out the light and we'll stand in total silence for a couple of minutes. Then I'll play the recording, and we'll see what happens."

When Ranger Eleni cut off the light, Amelia Bedelia gasped. It was so dark! Luckily the moon was almost full. Soon her eyes adjusted to the moonlight and she started to make out things, like Ranger Eleni's hat and Cliff standing next to her. She looked for Candy but didn't spot her.

It was really dark, and there were

creepy shadows everywhere. She could feel herself wanting to fidget, so she willed herself to stand completely still.

Eleni started the recording of owl calls. Soon, a strange shrill sound echoed through the trees all around them. The sound made everyone huddle close together, even though they knew it was just a recording. Amelia Bedelia held her breath. She really hoped they would see an owl.

Suddenly Ranger Eleni switched on the spotlight. And there, on a nearby branch, sat a small owl. Amelia Bedelia hadn't even heard it arrive. It looked more like a cute feathered robot than an actual bird. It had a thin beak and stared at them with large, unblinking eyes.

"Awwww," someone said, forgetting they were supposed to be quiet. All of a sudden there was a horrible sound, very close by. A drawn-out piercing scream, like someone was in terrible pain. Ranger Eleni spun the spotlight around. And right above their heads, Amelia Bedelia saw a large white face.

"What was that?" someone shouted.

Ranger Eleni shined her light around the clearing to make sure everyone was safe. "Everyone okay?" she asked. "What a bonus! That was a barn owl. You almost never see them in the woods. They're mostly found in fields. And in graveyards too. They sound just like a person screaming."

"I thought it was a ghost," whispered Angel.

Ranger Eleni trained her light on the ground, then knelt down to grab something. "What is this?" she asked, holding it up.

Amelia Bedelia and her friends gasped. Ranger Eleni held a bright red apple in her hand.

The ghost was back!

That was when Ranger Eleni's spotlight went out. The clearing was plunged into darkness again.

"Oh no," the ranger said. "Hold on a second while I get my flashlight."

Clip-clop, clip-clop, clip-clop.

Cliff grabbed Amelia Bedelia's arm.

"Are you hearing what I'm hearing?" he whispered.

Amelia Bedelia nodded, her heart beating fast.

Clip-clop, clip-clop, clip-clop.

"It's the ghost!" Skip yelled.

Ranger Eleni turned on her flashlight. Amelia Bedelia could see the terrified faces of her classmates. She was sure hers looked the same.

"Calm down," said Ms. Garcia. "I know you all have Halloween on the brain, but this is ridiculous. Clearly someone is riding a horse nearby."

"That's odd," said Ranger Eleni. "I've never heard a horse here before."

The friends were quiet on the walk

back to the parking lot. They piled onto the bus silently.

"What's wrong, campers?" asked Ms. Chang. "You all look like you've seen a ghost!"

"No, but we sure heard one," said Amelia Bedelia.

AN APPLE A DAY . . .

"Ready, pumpkin?" Amelia Bedelia's mother called from the living room.

"Ready!" said Amelia Bedelia. She and Finally raced downstairs. After trial and error, she had designed a costume that Finally would actually wear. Her dog was dressed as a pirate, complete with eye patch.

"Ta-da!" shouted Amelia Bedelia.

"Well, blow me down," said her mother. "Finally is the cutest pirate to ever sail the seven seas."

"Shiver me timbers, sweetie," said her father. "You two look terrific. But why aren't you a pirate too?"

Amelia Bedelia shrugged. "I couldn't find any pirate gear for myself, so I decided to go as the next best thing. A cat."

Amelia Bedelia's parents were dressed as ghosts. They were draped in white sheets with holes cut out for the eyes.

They were on their way to the Halloween celebration, which started in the park. Amelia Bedelia couldn't wait to play haunted mini-golf, jump in the bouncy house with her friends, stick her hands into gross things in the mad scientist's laboratory, make some arts and crafts, eat some snacks, and of course, carve the pumpkin that her father now held in his ghostly arms.

Amelia Bedelia grabbed her trick-or-treat bag. At the very last minute she spotted her small, cute pumpkin sitting on the coffee table. It looked sort of lonely, so she dropped it in her bag. She didn't want to leave it all by itself, especially on Halloween.

When they arrived at the park, kids and parents and pets were already milling around. Amelia Bedelia spotted Joy right away. She was wearing a cow costume with wings on her back and a halo over her head. Amelia Bedelia still didn't get it until her father spoke up.

"Holy cow!" he said. "What a clever costume!"

Amelia Bedelia spotted Alex and Alexandra (bacon and egg) from dance class and was happy to see Alice (in Wonderland) from camp (and the Upcycling Art Studio). Then she felt a hand clamp down on her shoulder. She spun around.

"Eek!" she screamed. It was Candy. Her face was painted a sickly green, with huge dark circles under her eyes, and she had a big gash across her cheek. Her hair was matted and had leaves stuck in it, and her clothing was torn and dirty.

"You look amazing!" said Amelia Bedelia. "Do you want to try the mad scientist's laboratory?"

Candy shook her undead head. "Kid stuff," she said, limping off in the direction of the mummy wrap tent.

Amelia Bedelia shrugged and headed straight to the laboratory. Ms. Garcia was wearing a splattered lab coat, a purple wig, elbow-length black rubber gloves, and goggles. She stood in front of a large rack filled with bubbling test tubes. "Enter my laboratory—if you dare!" she said. Amelia Bedelia giggled. On the lab table was a series of boxes. Each had a hole cut into the top, so that you could stick your hand inside.

The first was labeled INTESTINES. Amelia Bedelia bravely stuck her hand into what felt like a pile of slimy, long, thin worms. *Spaghetti*, she thought. EYEBALLS were next. The slick orbs felt a lot like peeled grapes to her. TEETH were candy corn, she was pretty sure.

But what was in the BRAINS box? She stuck her hand in once, then twice, trying to figure it out. Ms. Garcia noticed the puzzled look on her face. "Mashed potatoes," she whispered.

After she had wiped off her hands, Amelia Bedelia headed over to the arts and crafts tent, where she twisted pipe cleaners around a lollipop to make a spider pop and tried her hand at an origami monster bookmark. Then she wandered over to the bouncy house. She was about to take off her sneakers and get in line when Cliff ran by. "Grab your pumpkins and your adult supervision!" he hollered. "The pumpkin carving contest is about to begin!"

Amelia Bedelia found her parents and grabbed her pumpkin from her dad. Several tables were arranged under a big orange-and-black–striped tent, with lots of different tools lined up by each workstation. There were knives of various shapes and sizes, tooth saws, sculpting tools, scrapers, scoopers, etching tools, circle punches, and pumpkin drills.

Amelia Bedelia rolled up her cat sleeves. She quickly removed the top of her pumpkin and was soon elbow-deep in pumpkin guts. She thinned the walls of her pumpkin with a scraper and then started on the face. She had decided to carve a ghoulish expression with a big wide mouth full of jagged teeth. Under her parents' watchful gaze she worked on the eyes and nose, then moved on to the mouth.

"Can I borrow that pumpkin drill?" called Dawn from the other side of the table.

"Sure!" Amelia Bedelia called back.

Dawn headed over to retrieve it. But she rolled over a little more quickly than she had intended on her new skates. She was headed straight for Amelia Bedelia! Amelia Bedelia jumped out of the way, knocking her pumpkin to the ground.

"Sorry!" said Dawn. "I'm sorry!"

Amelia Bedelia picked up her pumpkin and gasped. A huge chunk had been knocked out! The mouth was now three times wider on one side than the other. Amelia Bedelia stared at her ruined pumpkin.

"Oh, too bad, sweetie," said her mother.

Skip looked up, peering through his astronaut helmet. "Tough break, Amelia Bedelia," he said. He grimaced. "Geez, there's practically room for another pumpkin inside that mouth!"

Amelia Bedelia smiled. Another pumpkin! She reached into her trick-or-treat bag and pulled out her cute little pumpkin. She held it up to her big pumpkin's gaping mouth. It would fit! She grabbed a marker and drew a tiny frightened face on it. Then she tucked it into her jack-o'-lantern's mouth. Perfect!

"Great save!" said her father. "The big pumpkin is eating the little pumpkin! Amelia Bedelia, that's amazing!"

Apparently the judges thought so too. Amelia Bedelia won for Most Creative.

After the contest, Amelia Bedelia wandered through the crowd, looking for Candy. She hoped her friend was having as good a time as she was.

She needn't have worried. She found Candy posing with props at the Halloween photo booth. They took a ton of silly pictures together. Afterward, they headed over to the snack table, where they sampled cake pops that looked like eyeballs and bright green cookie sandwiches called Monster Molars, with white marshmallow teeth in the middle. The cookies were messy but very tasty.

Amelia Bedelia noticed that people were beginning to hurry off, all in the same direction. "Come on!" she said to Candy. "It's time for the costume parade!" The two girls headed to the parade start, collecting their friends along the way. As they began to march, Cliff made up a song on the spot and began to sing it to the tune of "Yankee Doodle Dandy." Pretty soon all the kids in the parade joined in.

Halloween, oh Halloween
You are both fun and scary!
We dress in costumes, fangs, or masks
Like werewolves who are hairy!
Halloween, you are the best
(Almost as good as Christmas).
We'll trick-or-treat all over town
For stuff that's not nutritious!

Amelia Bedelia stole a glance at Candy. She was laughing and singing along with everyone else. "You were right!" Candy said. "This is so much fun!"

Then it was time to trick-or-treat! Almost every house was decorated. It was starting to get dark, so the jack-o'-lanterns on the porches were glowing. Amelia Bedelia and her friends took Candy to all the best houses, as they had promised.

When they were done, every bag was bulging at the seams.

Amelia Bedelia and Candy found their parents chatting together. Candy's mom immediately started digging through Candy's bag. "Jelly beans!" she said. "My favorite." She ripped open the box and started snacking. "Do you have any more?"

Candy looked. "Nope," she said.

"Here, let me look." Candy's mom

lifted her daughter's trick-or-treat bag. "This is way more candy than you usually collect!" she exclaimed. "Good thing you've been eating all those apples lately." She turned to Amelia Bedelia's parents. "We've practically gone through a bushel this week!"

A bushel of apples! That was a lot of apples. *Aha!* thought Amelia Bedelia.

Suddenly the scariest part of their scary stories made a lot of sense.

. . . KEEPS THE GHOSTS AWAY

"See you at Seven Gables Farm!" Amelia Bedelia and her friends called to one another as they piled into their cars.

Amelia Bedelia's father slipped off his ghost costume before getting behind the wheel, but her mother kept hers on. "I'm ready for that bonfire," she said, rubbing her chilly hands together.

When they arrived, the bonfire was already roaring. Mr. and Mrs. Hawthorne were handing out cups of hot cider to everyone. Mrs. Hawthorne greeted Amelia Bedelia with a big hug.

"Your costume is *purr-fect*!" she said. She looked Amelia Bedelia in the eye. "Can I trust you not to spill the beans?" she asked.

"Yup, Candy's mom already ate them all," Amelia Bedelia replied.

Mrs. Hawthorne leaned forward and whispered in her ear.

Amelia Bedelia smiled and nodded. "Your secret is safe with me," she said.

And then Amelia Bedelia knew exactly what she had to do.

She found Candy standing near the bonfire. She grabbed her hand. "Candy, I need you!" she said. "Finally ran into the corn maze! You've got to help me find her! I'm afraid she'll be lost forever!" She crossed her fingers behind her back as she said it.

"Oh no!" said Candy. "Come on!"

Amelia Bedelia and Candy raced into the maze. The full moon ducked behind some clouds just as they made their first turn. It was dark and creepy. A sudden breeze made the cornstalks rustle.

"Finally!" called Amelia Bedelia. "Here, girl!"

127

"Finally!" called Candy. "Where could she be?"

They reached the middle of the maze, and Amelia Bedelia stopped. The clouds parted. Candy's green zombie face looked especially spooky in the moonlight.

Candy glanced up. "A full moon," she said. "I hope it doesn't summon the ghost of Ebenezer!"

"Me too," said Amelia Bedelia.

"Why did we stop?" asked Candy. "We need to find your dog!"

Amelia Bedelia cocked her head. "Did you hear that?" she asked.

"Hear what?" said Candy.

"That!" whispered Amelia Bedelia.

Clip-clop, clip-clop, clip-clop.

Candy froze. "But that's impossible!" she said. "I mean, it can't be the horse from—" She turned to Amelia Bedelia. "Can it?"

"Let's find out," said Amelia Bedelia. "Follow me." She put her right hand on the maze wall, as her mother had taught her, and started walking. Soon they reached the end of the maze. They looked out across the shadowy pumpkin field.

Clip-clop, clip-clop, clip-clop.

Candy grabbed Amelia Bedelia's hand and squeezed it tight.

Clip-clop, clip-clop, clip-clop.

A horse-drawn wagon appeared, driven by a werewolf, its eyes glowing red in its furry face!

Candy gasped. She stared at Amelia Bedelia with her eyes wide.

Then it was so quiet that all Amelia Bedelia could hear was the snap and crackle of the bonfire. A screech owl screamed in the distance.

Mrs. Hawthorne broke the silence. "Welcome home!" she shouted. "Everyone, it's Sean! Howl's it going?"

"Surprise!" shouted the werewolf. "Happy Halloween, everybody!"

The crowd around the bonfire laughed. Sean took off his mask and jumped down from the wagon to hug his grandparents. "I couldn't miss Halloween at Seven Gables Farm," he said. "I hopped on a train as soon as I finished my exams. I rounded up some of my friends, and the haunted hayride is on!"

The crowd cheered.

Amelia Bedelia looked over at Candy, who was grinning at her.

"You got me, and you got me good!" Candy said. "When did you know it was me who was haunting our class?"

"When your mom talked about all the apples you kept taking," said Amelia Bedelia. "And when did *you* know that we were making up the ghost stories?"

"Well, you started off with a main character named Ebenezer Scrooge. Just like the guy from *A Christmas Carol*," Candy explained. "That's one of my favorites. You know, all the ghosts."

"Oh yeah. That's why I changed his

last name from Scrooge to Sludge," said Amelia Bedelia. She thought for a minute. "But how did you make those hoofbeats at the owl walk?"

Candy just smiled mysteriously. "I'll tell you *next* Halloween," she said.

"Hey, did you say *next* Halloween?" Amelia Bedelia asked excitedly. "Does that mean you're staying?"

Candy looked puzzled.

"Holly heard you tell Mrs. Shauk that maybe you should go back to Chicago," Amelia Bedelia explained.

"I meant for Halloween weekend!" said Candy. "Not forever! It's a good thing I didn't go. I had the best Halloween ever, right here. Where else would my friends make up a ghost story just for me and end the night by scaring my pants off?"

"I'm glad you had such a great time," said Amelia Bedelia. "But we'd better find them right away. It can get very chilly on the haunted hayride. Especially without your pants!"

TWO WAYS TO SAY IT

Not in my book!

Not according to me!

Just what the doctor ordered!

Exactly what I wanted!

Spit it out!

Start talking!

I don't give a hoot.

I don't care about that.

136

I can't keep a straight face. **The way I feel shows up on my face.**

I bought it for a song. **I got it for a low price.**

You bet your boots! **It's certain!**

I'm not falling for that. **You're not going to trick me.**

You look like you've seen a ghost. **You look really shocked.**

Spill the beans! **Tell me the secret!**

Monstrously

Supplies:

- Square origami paper (or any foldable paper cut into a six-inch square)
- paper scraps
- markers

Tools:

- glue stick
- scissors

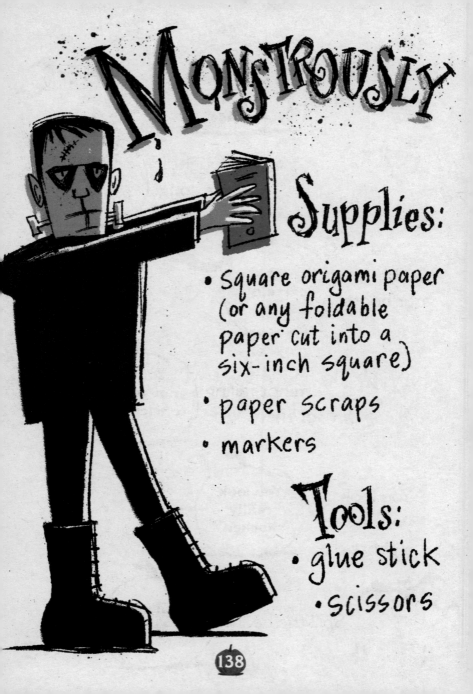

Fun Bookmarks

Directions:

1  Take the square piece of paper and fold it in half (point to point) to make a triangle.

2 With the middle point facing up, take the right corner and fold up toward the middle point.

3 Then do the same to the left corner so they meet in the center.

 **4** After you have creased these edges, open them back up to form a triangle again.

5 Pull the top layer of the middle point down so the tip touches the center of the flat bottom edge.

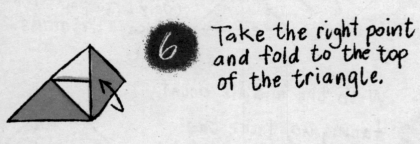

6 Take the right point and fold to the top of the triangle.

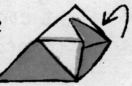

7 Then fold it into the pouch at the bottom.

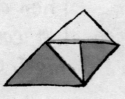

8 Tuck inside, and crease the edge. 140

9 Do the same with the left corner.

10 Turn the bookmark around, so the folded side is on top.

11 Decorate the folded side of the pouch with as many details as you like. You can glue on eyes, spots, or teeth; color the inside of the mouth; add fangs or one snaggle tooth - whatever you want! Color the eyes and any other details with the markers.

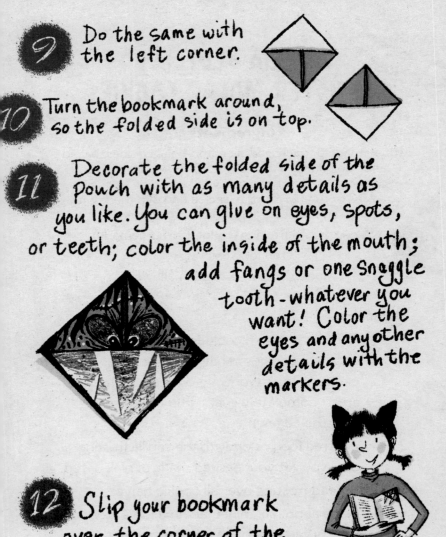

12 Slip your bookmark over the corner of the page of the book you are reading, to save your place!

AMELIA BEDELIA'S
MONSTER MOLAR COOKIES

Ingredients

Homemade or packaged slice-and-bake cookies, baked
and cooled (any flat round cookies will do—sugar,
oatmeal, chocolate chip. If you prefer, make sugar
cookies from your favorite recipe and dye them with
green food coloring. That's even better!)

½ cup vanilla frosting (canned or homemade)

red food coloring

about 1 cup mini marshmallows

Directions

1. When the baked cookies are completely
    cool, cut cookies in half to make two half
    circles. (Don't worry if your half circles
    aren't completely even. The frosting will
    hide the edges.)

2. Add red food coloring to the vanilla frosting
    until you get your desired shade of pink or red.

3. Spread frosting over all cookie halves.

4. Place about six mini marshmallows around
    the curved part of half of the cookies.

5. Cover with the other half of a cookie
    to make a mouth.

ENJOY!

142

SPIDER POPS

Supplies (for each spider)
2 black pipe cleaners
1 round lollipop, wrapped
2 googly eyes
Tools
glue
scissors

Directions

1. Cut pipe cleaners in half.

2. Line pipe cleaners up on table.

3. Place lollipop on top of pipe cleaners. Lie it down so the center of the pipe cleaners is at the top of the stick, right under the candy.

4. Fold pipe cleaners over the stick, first one side, then the other.

5. Flip lollipop over.

6. Separate the pipe-cleaner legs and fold down the last ½ inch at the ends so the spider can stand up.

7. Put glue on the backs of the googly eyes.

8. Glue the googly eyes onto the pipe cleaner in front, farthest away from the lollipop.

The Amelia Bedelia Chapter Books

1. Amelia Bedelia Means Business
by Herman Parish   pictures by Lynne Avril

2. Amelia Bedelia Unleashed
by Herman Parish   pictures by Lynne Avril

3. Amelia Bedelia Road Trip!
by Herman Parish   pictures by Lynne Avril

4. Amelia Bedelia Goes Wild!
by Herman Parish   pictures by Lynne Avril

5. Amelia Bedelia Shapes Up
by Herman Parish   pictures by Lynne Avril

6. Amelia Bedelia Cleans Up
by Herman Parish   pictures by Lynne Avril

Have you read them all?

Introducing...
Amelia Bedelia
& FRIENDS

Amelia Bedelia + Good Friends =
Super Fun Stories
to Read and Share

Amelia Bedelia and her friends celebrate their school's birthday.

Amelia Bedelia and her friends discover a stray kitten on the playground!

Amelia Bedelia and her friends
take a school trip to the Middle
Ages that is as different as
knight and day.

Amelia Bedelia and
her friends work
to save Earth and
beautify their town.

Amelia Bedelia and
her friends win an
ice cream party.

Coming
soon . . .

Amelia Bedelia and her
friends have a sleepover
that is out of this world!

Amelia Bedelia springs into action in this funny story about good eggs and busy bees.

Amelia Bedelia

Hops to It

BY HERMAN PARISH   PICTURES BY LYNNE AVRIL

Get ready to read

Amelia Bedelia

Hops to It

coming just in time for Easter 2022!